Published by
Delacorte Press
Bantam Doubleday Dell Publishing Group, Inc.
666 Fifth Avenue
New York, New York 10103

This edition was first published in Great Britain by Methuen Children's Books.

ISBN: 0–385–30431–5 ISBN: 0–385–30432–3 (lib. bdg.)
Library of Congress Cataloging in Publication Data will
appear in subsequent editions.

Manufactured in Singapore

September 1991
10 9 8 7 6 5 4 3 2 1

JENNY *and* BOB

by David Wynn Millward
pictures by Kady MacDonald Denton

Delacorte Press

Angry Jenny

Jenny was angry with cat.

Cat hid.

Jenny was angry with dolly.

Dolly broke.

Jenny was angry with Mommy.

Mommy sent her to bed.

Jenny cried.
Then she felt better.

She stroked cat.

She mended dolly.

"Sorry, Mommy," said Jenny.

Poor Bird

"Bird is dead," said Bob.

"No," said Jenny.
"Bird is sleeping."

"Wake up, bird."

"Bird is dead," said Bob.

"Poor bird," said Jenny.

"Let's bury bird," said Jenny.

"Yes," said Bob.

"Go away, cat," said Jenny.

"Poor bird," said Bob.

"Cat will guard you."

Rainy Day

"Rain again," said Jenny.
"Let's play," said Bob.

"Slickers on," said Mom.

"This puddle is a lake."

"This puddle is the sea."

"Here's a boat."

"Here's a ship."

"We are GIANTS!"

SPLISH SPLASH

"Goodbye, lake," said Jenny.
"Goodbye, sea," said Bob.